BEYOND HEAVEN
CHICAGO HOUSE PARTY FLYERS
VOLUME II, FROM 1981-1992

*All archival materials courtesy of donation
by the collection of*

Mario "Liv it up" Luna
Chicago

BEYOND HEAVEN: CHICAGO HOUSE PARTY FLYERS, VOLUME II, FROM 1981-1992
PUBLISHED BY ALMIGHTY & INSANE BOOKS
WWW.ALMIGHTYANDINSANEBOOKS.COM

FIRST EDITION, SECOND PRINTING
COPYRIGHT © 2023 ALMIGHTY & INSANE BOOKS
ISBN: 978-1-7345873-0-2

PRINTED IN CHINA BY PRINT NINJA, EVANSTON, IL
DESIGN: BRANDON JOHNSON

IMPORTES ETC......

711 S. Plymouth Ct.
Chicago, Ill. 60605
(312) 922-3143

CHICAGO'S TOP 25 DANCE MUSIC AS OF DECEMBER 16, 1983

ARTIST	TITLE
Sharon Redd	Love How You Feel/Winner/Activate
Shannon	Let The Music Play
P.McCartney/M.Jackson	Say, Say, Say
Loleatta Holloway	Love Sensation (RX)
Eartha Kitt	Where Is My Man
Lisa	Rocket To Your Heart
Cuba Gooding	Happiness Is Just Around The Bend
Lime	Angel Eyes/On The Grid (RX)
Freeez	Pop Goes My Love
Sheena Easton	Telefone
Charade	Got To Get To You
Hall & Oates	Say It Isn't So
Irene Cara	Why Me
Romantics	Talking In Your Sleep
Sarah Dash	Lucky Tonight
Culture Club	All Cuts (LP)
Stephanie Mills	Pilot Error
Jenny Burton	I Remember What You Like
Grand Master	White Lines
Madonna	Holiday/Lucky Star
LeJete	La Cage Aux Folles
Gloria Gaynor	I Am What I Am
Jefferey Osborne	Stay With Me Tonight
Pure Energy	Love Games
Three Million	I've Been Robbed

TOP DISCO----IMPORTES, ETC.

Torch Song	Prepare to Energize
World Premier	Share The Night
Inner Life	No Way
Creatures	Believe In Yourself (RX)
The Reel	Percussion (RX)
Laid Back	White Horse
Yello	Lost Again
Free Enterprise	Make It On My Own
Chi Chi-Liah	Bonus Beats
Koto	Japanese War Games
Steve Harvey	Tonight
Roland Rat	Rat Rapping
Lilly Ann	Goin' Crazy
X-Ray Connection	Get Ready
Master Genious	Let's Break
George Kranz	Trommeltanz (Din Dah Dah)
Cerrone	Where Are You Now
Barbra Mason	Another Man
Flirtations	Earth Quake
Jamican Girls	Love Somebody New
Art Of Noise	Beat Box
Indeep	Records Keep On Spinning
Innerlife	Ain't No Mountain High Enough
Nick Straker	Against The Wall
Hot Box	Do You Want A Latin Lover
Jenny Burton	I Remember What You Like
Freeez	We Got The Juice (LP Cut)
Kreamcicle	No News Is New
First Choice	Dr. Love (RX)
Baricentra	Tittle Tattle
Cock Roach	Get Back
Smiles	Pendulum
T.S.O.P.	Philadelphia
Firefly	Love Is Coming/Your Door

S E A S O N S   G R E E T I N G S !

IMPORTES ETC......

711 S. Plymouth Ct.
Chicago, Ill. 60605
(312) 922-3143

CHICAGO'S TOP 25 DANCE MUSIC AS OF DECEMBER 5, 1983

ARTIST	TITLE
Shannon	Let The Music Play
Sharon Redd	I Love How You Feel
McCartney/Jackson	Say, Say, Say
Lime	Angel Eyes
Lisa	Rocket To Your Heart
Sheena Easton	Telefone
Stephanie Mills	Pilot Error
Loleatta Holloway	Love Sensation
Le Jete	La Cage Aux Folles
Eartha Kitt	Where Is My Man
Freeez	Pop Goes My Love
Cuba Gooding	Happiness Is Just Around The Bend
Culture Club	All Cuts (LP)
Romantics	Talking In Your Sleep
Sarah Dash	Lucky Tonight
Charade	Got To Get To You
Quando Quango	Love Tempo
Madonna	Holiday/Lucky Star
Irene Cara	Why Me?
Gary's Gang	Makin' Music
Take Three	Tonight (Alright)
Grand Master Flash	Whitelines
Gloria Gaynor	I Am What I Am
Pointer Sisters	I Need You
Gwen Jonae	Destiny

TOP DISCO----IMPORTES, ETC.

ARTIST	TITLE
Sharon Redd	All Cuts (LP)
Xena	On The Upside
George Kranz	Trommeltanz (Din Dah Dah)
Chi Chi-Liah	Bonus Beats/Proud Mary
Free Enterprise	Make It On My Own
Jenny Burton	I Remember What You Like
The Reel	Percussion
Art Of Noise	Beat Box
Yello	Lost Again
Creatures	Believe In Yourself (RX)
Freeez	We Got The Jazz (LP Cut)
Gaz Nevada	Special Agent Man
Koto	Japanese War Games
Inner Life	No Way
Jamican Girls	Love Somebody New
Whodini	Yours For The Night
Flirtations	Earth Quake
Barbara Mason	Another Man
James Ingram	You May Be There
X-Ray Connection	Get Ready
Lilly Ann	Goin' Crazy
Cerrone	Where Are You Now
Master Genious	Let's Break
Let's Disco	Rhythm Traxs - RARE!!
Roland Rat	Rat Rapping
Laid Back	White Horse
Lisa	Manipitory Love/Sex Dance
Steve Harvey	Tonight
Brooklyn Express	Love Is The Message
Kreamcicle	No News Is News
Broads	Sing, Sing, Sing
Sharon Brown	You Got Me Where I Want To Be
Loleatta Holloway	Love Sensation
Nightmoves	Transdance (COME BACK)

INTRODUCTION

Chicago is the birthplace of house music. Along with unique styles of blues and jazz, house is one of the city's greatest and most influential global musical exports. The genre first found its sound in a gay, black, post-disco culture of the late 1970s within the walls of underground clubs, most famously the Warehouse (located at 206 S. Jefferson Street in Chicago's West Loop) where Frankie Knuckles practiced a style of DJing that blended disco, soul, funk, R&B, rock, reggae, post-punk—a little bit of "literally everything" to quote Knuckles—from 1977 to 1983. Meanwhile, friend and fellow DJ Ron Hardy was doing his thing at a club called Den One in Old Town, later becoming resident at Muzic Box where he featured in his sets many reel-to-reel edits and rhythm tracks on acetate. The exchange between these two DJs (who attended each other's club nights) created a sound that influenced local producers including Jesse Saunders, Vince Lawrence, Marshall Jefferson, Larry Heard, Steve "Silk" Hurley, Adonis, Farley "Jackmaster" Funk, Lil Louis, Chip E., and Phuture (to name a few) to begin recording original tracks using the newly-developed Roland TR-808 and TB-303 drum machines to put underlying grooves beneath it all. While unofficial releases such as Jamie Principle's "Your Love" were circulating Chicago's clubs by the early 1980s, many recognize the first official Chicago house record to be pressed on vinyl as Jesse Saunders "On and On" released by Jes Say Records in early 1984. From there the recording movement caught fire, with records being released by Trax, DJ International, Mitchbal, IHR, Hot Mix 5, and other independent labels, including labels like Jes Say Records founded by the artists themselves.

In sourcing their material, many first-generation house DJs went to Importes, Etc. located in a garage on Printers Row in the south Loop, and its main competitor, Loop Records—a mile away on State Street. Importes, Etc. was the first record store to designate a specific section for house music. There are multiple origin stories for the term "house" and each of the genre's originators seem to have their own explanation. While some say the name came from the music being created at home, or from the type of records being played at home, the general consensus is that "house" is a shortening of Warehouse—"The House" being a nickname of the club where Frankie Knuckles was resident. This designation at Importes, Etc. made it easier for customers searching for records being played at the Warehouse, later adding original vinyl pressings by Chicago's own house artists as new releases rolled out and interest in the burgeoning movement grew.

Besides clubs and record stores, the primary and most far-reaching outlet for popularizing house music was the Chicagoland radio station WBMX, with its Hot

Mix 5 DJs doing live mixes on the air to a listener base of a million people per week. The original Hot Mix 5 lineup consisted of Mickey "Mixin" Oliver, Farley "Funkin" Keith (later known as Farley "Jackmaster" Funk), Scott "Smokin" Silz, Ralphi "Rockin" Rosario, and Kenny "Jammin" Jason, with Julian "Jumpin" Perez later replacing Scott Silz in 1984. The Hot Mix 5 featured at many clubs and halls, together or individually, throughout the 1980s. WBMX and the Hot Mix 5 were instrumental to bringing house music from the clubs into Chicago's mainstream, and from there to other cities in the U.S., Europe, and beyond.

This book catalogs a collection of flyers and other house-related ephemera from the years 1981 to 1992, courtesy of Mario "Liv It Up" Luna, a DJ living in the Pilsen neighborhood of Chicago during this time. These flyers, also known as pluggers, were used for promotional purposes. They would be placed in record stores and passed out at schools and on the street to help get the word out about upcoming house music parties and events. Although by no means encyclopedic, this flyer collection documents a variety of figures from Chicago's emerging house scene: first-generation DJs and producers, the WBMX Hot Mix 5, and other lesser-known DJs at different venues across the city. Also in the mix are promoters, record stores, labels, and an assortment of party crews and dance groups who contributed to the growth and atmosphere of house music in Chicago. These flyers give a taste of what many consider to be the best times of their lives, and for others acts as a gateway to a golden era in the history of Chicago music.

CODA

This volume is a continuation of the Beyond Heaven house music flyers project. Since the first book was released, Mario "Liv It Up" Luna uncovered a significant amount of forgotten yet equally important material from his collection. Due to all the love expressed for the original, we determined this additional content to be worthy of its own new volume. The format remains the same, and the text above is still valid. Given the global popularity and historical importance of house music in this day and age, we believe it is essential to preserve and share this archive with those who will appreciate and learn from it now and in the future. Once again, we'll end with this: Long Live House!

The Chicago BAD BOYS

-PRESENT-

the 1989 HOUSE CONVENTION

AT THE EXCLUSIVE
— MARRIOT HOTEL —
540 N. MICHIGAN AVE.

FRIDAY, DECEMBER 29TH

DOORS OPEN AT 7:00 P.M.
ADMISSION: $8.00 UNTIL 9:00 P.M.
MUSIC BY CHICAGO'S BEST

PHARRIS THOMAS
(Raquetball Club)

TERRY HUNTER
(Sauer's)

ARMANDO
(Bismarck)

GENE HUNT
(Res Hall, Divinci)

— WITH SPECIAL GUESTS —

FRANKIE KNUCKLES, **LIL' LOUIS,** **RON HARDY**
(VIA N.Y. CITY) (FRENCH KISS) (MUZIC BOX)

THIS EVENT WILL BE HOSTED BY:

WGCI'S **Doug Banks**   ALONG WKKC'S **Pink House**

SPECIAL NOTE: THIS EVENT WILL NOT BE
CANCELLED UNDER ANY CIRCUMSTANCES !!!
P.S.: DON'T FORGET ABOUT LEO H.S.
FRIDAY, DECEMBER 22nd " THE BLACKOUT PARTY".
FOR MORE INFO CALL: 779-0865, 854-0871, 854-0315,
791-1654, 521-6300.
THIS IS A 1989
* CHICAGO BAD BOYS PRODUCTION *

SUNDAY SEPT. 1st
PRE-LABOR DAY
BACK TO SCHOOL
SMORGASBOARD
POWER PLANT
2210 S. MICHIGAN
9:00 UNTIL
RON HARDY

J.N.S. GRAND PRODUCTION
presents
"Spring Spin-Off 85"

ARAGON Ballroom
1106 W. Lawrence
Saturday May 25, '85

FEATURING:

Larry "Lollipop" Anderson
(From Snuggery)

Terry "Mixin" Mack

Tony "Boom Boom" Badea
(From W.J.P.C.)

Butch Salinas
(From Nightlife Unlimited)

Mark Imperial
(From Dilligaf's)

Tim Schommer
(From Tom Foolery's)

SPECIAL GUEST FROM W.B.M.X.
MICKEY "MIXIN" OLIVER
FARLEY "JACK MASTER" FUNK
RALPHI "ROCKIN" ROSARIO

ADMISSION: $8.00 **7:30 P.M.**

* SPECIAL GUEST JUDGES *

Jaime Principle	Lauren Alcarese	Frankie "Hollywood" Rodriguez	Roger Vergara
(Artist, Persona Records)	(From Audio Talent)	(Master Mixer From W.G.C.I.)	(From High Society)

GET YOUR TICKETS **NOW** FOR THE HOTTEST D.J. CONTEST
TICKETS AVAILABLE AT ALL TICKET MASTER OUTLETS OR CALL: **559-1212**.
● TICKETS ALSO AVAILABLE AT THE DOOR ● ALL AGES ADMITTED ●
● SECURITY PROVIDED ● COME PARTY WITH US!! ●

PRINTED BY PRONTO PRINTING SERVICE ● 4152 W. NORTH AVE. CHICAGO, ILL. 60639 ● TEL. (312) 486-9289

COME CHECK OUT
D.J. INTERNATIONAL'S

 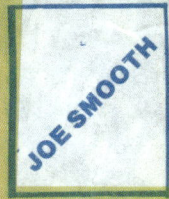 

TYREE COOPER — **JOE SMOOTH** — **FAST EDDIE**

AS THEY MAKE THEIR LAST CHICAGO APPEARANCE AND PREPARE FOR THEIR

LONDON—ENGLAND TOUR.

AND GET A TASTE OF
CHICAGO'S INDIANA'S AND BLUE ISLAND'S VERY OWN...

MARTIN "BOOGIE MAN" LUNA   MARIO "NON—STOP" NIEVES   "RADICAL" JESSE MENDOZA

PONY BOY   RALPHIE Z.

JOSE "TRUE BEAT" RODRIGUEZ   XAVIER QUINTANA

FREE   PARTY   GIVEAWAY

THE SCHOOL WITH THE MOST H.S. I.D.'S SHOWN AT THIS PARTY WILL WIN FREE D.J. SERVICES, INCLUDING: D.J.'S LIGHTS AND SOUND. FOR MORE DETAILS ASK YOUR PROM COMMITEE OR SCHOOL REPRESENTATIVES.

NANDY VIRAMONTES —WITH SPECIAL GUEST— PETER "Action" AMBRIZ
RUDY HERRERA   LOUIE RAMIREZ   HUGO ROGRIGUEZ   JIMMY "SPEEDY" G.
BABY "O"   PHIL CLAY   RAUL ORTIZ   JEFF LUCERO   D.J. ANDY A.

FRI. NOV. 25th, '88

AT CHICAGO'S PARTY HEADQUARTERS

UNION HALL

FROM 6 P.M. TO 6 A.M.
9350 SOUTH CHICAGO AVE.

$4 W/F OR H.S. I.D. — $5 W/O
AFTER $5 W/F OR H.S. I.D. — $6 W/O

APOLLO SECURITY
PROV. INSIDE OUT

ATTENTION ALL TEENS: WE BRING YOU MIX MASTERS NIGHT AT THE HOTTEST TEEN CLUB EVERY SUNDAY STARTING NOV. 20th

AT **JUMP STREET** 1052 INDIANAPOLIS BLVD., INDIANA
FEATURING: MARTIN BOOGIE MAN LUNA   RADICAL JESSE MENDOZA   NOEY MADMIXIN MORIN

FLYERS AVAIL. AT:
SULEMA'S HAIR PROVISIONS   PETES SERVICE STATION
3114 E. 83RD   2863 E. 95TH

LOOP RECORDS   J.T.'S   IMPORTS ETC.
320 S. STATE   2639 W. 95TH   711 S. PLYMOUTH

FRI. APRIL 29TH

GUCCI & DJR PROMOTIONS

BRINGING YOU THE FIRST OF IT'S KIND

$500.00
DA BUTT CONTEST

DO DA BUTT WITH YOUR FRIEND, YOUR FREAK, OR YOURSELF. IF YOU GOT A BIG BUTT, SMALL BUTT, ANY KINDA BUTT COME OUT, DO DA BUTT AND GET PAID.................$

BUTT MUSIC BY..................

RON HARDY
PHARRIS TERRY
SHANNON

MY HOUSE

87TH & ASHLAND
8PM TIL 2 AM
$6.00 ALL NITE

BE THERE

AN '88 GUCCI & DJR PROMOTION

DADDY'S COMIN...
"4"
THE EASTER W...
LIL LOU...

THE DADDY OF HOUS...
WILL BE IN CHICA...

SAT. APRIL...

EASTER EVE...
DOWNTOWN AT...

BISMAR...

PAVILION...
171 W. RANDOL...
7 P.M. – 2...
TO BE WITH HIS...
"U" R PART OF H...
THIS EVENT WILL BE...
$8.00 TIL 8:30 P.M. –...
P.S. YOU'D BETTER C...

DIAMOND CORP. '90

HOME

EKEND

JSIC

4th

T.

ILY
MILY
O TAPED
00 AFTER
 EARLY

IT'S TIME

WHAT TIME ???

TIME TO JACK

FRIDAY, FEBRUARY, 28th. 1986

LINCOLNWAY LODGE

230 S. Lincolnway (Rt. 31) Aurora

featuring

"HIT MAN"
MIKE WILSON

Music jacked from 7:00 until 1:00 A.M.

(M.A.W. D.J; ENTERPRISES & W.M.R.O.)

$3.00 W/F $4.00 W/O

Having a party to help a friend...

ARMANDO

Proceeds to help with hospital costs

music served up by Chicago's top DJ's

FARLEY
PHARRIS
MIKE DUNN
GENE HUNT
ANDRE HATCHETT
TERRY HUNTER

SUNDAY SEPT. 15

WAREHOUSE
nite club

738 W. RANDOLPH

Donation $10 • 21 & Over
ID's Required • 9pm - 4am

312.454.9004

Pronto Printing 312.486.9289

Westsides Hottest
D.J. TEAMS

ULTIMATE PARTY Crew	**MARIO** "Live it up" **LUNA** **RAPHAEL** "Ito" **GARCIA**
DIMENSIONAL Sounds	Jose "Guessman" Flores "Cutmaster" **CONRAD**
BRIDGEVIEW	**GEORGIO**

★ SOUTHSIDES VERY OWN ★
D.J. TEAMS

THEE BOYZ	**SLICK** "Scratchin" **RICK** "Rock The House" **ROD**
HARDCORE Slice	**MIKEY** "Power Play" **PAZ** **RAMARIO** "The Mastermix **MANZO**
LATIN BEATS	**JOSE** "The True Beat" **RODRIGUEZ**

GUEST D.J.'S

"Jumpin" J.
Steve "Boppin"
Bonilla
Mario "Nasty Boy" Luigi

Jimmie "Speedy" Gonzalez

Juan JackMaster Jock
Rompin Roy

Guill "Vicious" Velez
Lil Beto

RICHIES "Bad" ROBALINO

D.J.'S OF THE MIDWAY

JESSE "Jack The Beat" FLORES

RIGO "Mixman" MORENO
CISCO "The Beat"

LATIN BEATS
THEE BOYZ

BELIEVE IT!

AND SPINNING LIVE

WBMX
102.7 FM
SUPERMIX 6 VERY OWN

BAD BOY BILL
&
MIKE "Hitman" WILSON

WGCI 107.5 FM AM 1390
CHICAGO'S #1 MUSIC STATION

live

HOTMIX 5 VERY OWN

MICKEY "Mixin" OLIVER
&
JOHNNY "Wildboy" B.

insanity

CHICAGO'S GREAT BATTLE OF THE DANCE GROUPS

A.K.A.   **CULITOS**   **CONTACT**

IMPORTED TASTE   **ZODIAC DANCERS**

SAT AUG. 31, 85
USA RAINBO DISCO
4836 N CLARK
DOORS OPEN 8 PM TIL 3 AM

BISMARCK PAVILION
Downtown - Randolph at LaSalle

PARTY MASSACRE
Good Friday

Friday, April 17th • 7PM til

Don't Be Left Outside in that long line:

COME EARLY

WAREHOUSE & CLUBSTYLE FASHION SHOW - STYLES OF TODAY & TOMORROW

ARMANDO
D.J. from Medusa's

D.J. RUSH
D.J. from The PowerHouse

JAMILE PATTON
From the Loft

Mike Brown (Maywood) D.J. of the Northlake Parties also Eric Wade & Scott "B"

$8.00 w/p   Info: 488-0526
TLCC Productions

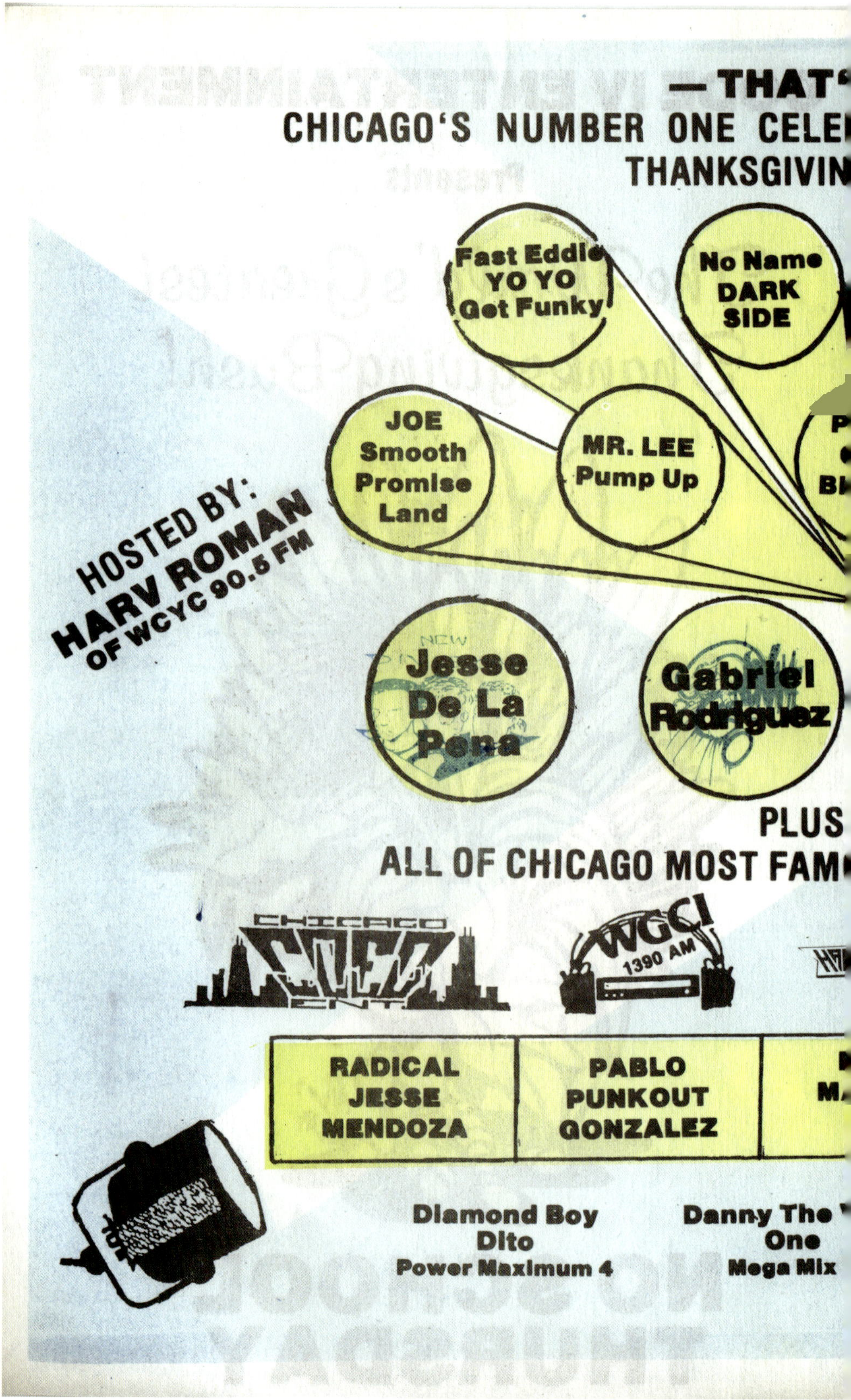

— THAT'
CHICAGO'S NUMBER ONE CELE
THANKSGIVIN

- Fast Eddie YO YO Get Funky
- No Name DARK SIDE
- JOE Smooth Promise Land
- MR. LEE Pump Up
- Jesse De La Pena
- Gabriel Rodriguez

HOSTED BY: HARV ROMAN OF WCYC 90.5 FM

PLUS
ALL OF CHICAGO MOST FAM

RADICAL JESSE MENDOZA	PABLO PUNKOUT GONZALEZ	

Diamond Boy Dito
Power Maximum 4

Danny The One
Mega Mix

HT —
S ARE HERE TO START THIS
BRATION.

- hite Boy MIKE
  Monkey Go
- Code of LACE Say You Love Me
- Entourage Thank You
- Georgie PORGIE Baby Come Back
- Mario on Stop Slaves
- Tony Boom Boom Badea

HOSTED BY:
DERRICK CARTER
89.3 FM. WNUR

BY
OBIL D.J. AND D.J. TEAMS

| ADAM ROCK | DELERIOUS DANNY |

Orlando Chavez
Dimensional Soounds

XAVIER QUINTANA
COED Ent.

UNO PRODUCTIONS
Invites You The Chosen and Priveledged few to Chicago's Frist and Last
2 Part Party

PART 1

12th Year Anniversary Party

for

HOUSE MUSIC

on

THANKSGIVING NITE THURSDAY NOV. 23rd

Downtown at **SAUERS**

311 E. 23rd

(around the corner from Heroes Night Club)

Featuring music by the originator, the Guy who started it all....

Adm. $8.00 w/invite
$10.00 w/o invite
7 p.m. til 2 a.m.

FRANKIE KNUCKLES

Guest School Host:
Kenwood H.S
For info.
225-6171

Coming VIA from N.Y.

Music also by:

MAURICE BROWN & GENE HUNT

P.S. This party is strictly for the IN CROWD, and the new generation party goers, which is you. Everything that happened way back when is over. UNO PROD. are bringing you new parties, new music, and most important new people for Chicago's party goers. So if you not with the IN CROWD, stay home.

"It's about time somebody celebrated the birth of house music, I don't know why it hasn't been done yet, and since it's UNO Productions Party, I know there will be thousands at the party, and I can't wait"- FRANKIE KNUCKLES.

and Present

EXPOSÉ   **EXPOSÉ**

LIVE IN CONCERT
THE HOTTEST GROUP OUT OF MIAMI
SINGING THER HIT SONG
POINT OF NO RETURN
SAT, OCT 19, 1985

DOORS OPEN AT 8:30   **AT THE RAINBO**   DOORS OPEN AT 8:30

4836 NORTH CLARK

DANCE PARTY TO FOLLOW

— FEATURING —

MICKEY" MIXIN" OLIVER
DON'T MISS THIS SUPER CONCERT AND DANCE PARTY

BI-LEVEL-DANCING   MAIN LEVEL ALL AGES
2nd LEVEL 21 and OVER

ADMISSION   ADVANCE TICKETS $7.00
W/CLUB IMAGEN CARD OR FLYER $9.00
PRICE AT DOOR $10.00

TICKETS AVAILABLE AT

   (TICKET INFO ON OTHER SIDE)
A TONY BITOY PRODUCTION

FOR MORE INFO PHONE 943-2347

&

INVITE YOU TO SEE **LIVE** PERFORMANCE BY:

Recording Stars

INTRODUCING...

Performing **"ESCAPE"**

Performing **"FASCINATION"** - **"Show You"**

Performing **"ALL THE TIME"**

PLUS MANY MORE **SOUND PAK** RECORDING STARS

ALSO SPECIAL GUEST
WHITE KNIGHT

AND CHICAGO'S GREATEST D.J.'S

CHARLIE "CHAZ" D.	**RICHIE "BAD" ROBALINO**
CHICAGO SUPREME D.J. TEAM	
MARTINO "SPINNIN" RAMOS	**MICKEY "D"**
CHICAGO SUPER MIX 6	
TOM "PUERTO RICAN" PEREZ	**"TOO COOL" KRIS**
PAUL BARREDA	**FERNANDO "NANDY" VIRAMONTES**
WILSON "VICIOUS" VEGA	**MARTIN "BOOGIEMAN" LUNA**

STEVE "SPINNIN" SANTOYO
(FROM WCRX)

Thurs. April 16, '87
AT
DANCING WHEELS

8,000 SQ. FT.
DANCE FLOOR
WITH A SPECTACULAR
LIGHT & SOUND
$6 W/FLYER
$7 W/O

4150 W. 55th ST.
P.S. NO SCHOOL FRIDAY!!

SECURITY PROVIDED — DOORS OPEN AT 7:30
ALL OF THIS IS BROUGHT TO YOU BY PAUL BARREDA — 436-5591

GEORGE FIERRO Productions **ALL NIGHT JAM Productions**

INVITE YOU TO ATTEND...

THE GREAT BATTLE OF THE SOUTHSIDE DANCE GROUPS

AS CHICAGO'S **TOP FOUR JACKIN' CREWS** GO HEADS UP FOR A **$200.00 CASH PRIZE**

Featuring

THE SEXX BOYZ & GIRLZ **NAUGHTY GIRLS**

ALL STARS (THE SEQUAL) **DESTINEE DANCERS**

BUT IF YOU THINK THAT IS ALL...YOU GOT ANOTHER THING COMMIN' THIS **WILD SET** WILL BE JACKED UP BY CHICAGO'S OWN...
TOM "Puerto Rico" **PEREZ, CHARLIE** "Chaz" **D., RICHIE'S** "Bad" **ROBALINO, SMOKIN'** D.J., **C.C., WILSON** "Vicious" **VEGA, RAUL GONZALEZ**
SO IF YOU DON'T WANT TO BE ALONE ON **SAT. THE 14TH**, COME AND PARTY WITH OVER **500** OF CHICAGO'S PARTY ANIMALS AND JUDGE FOR YOURSELF WHO'S **REALLY NO. 1**

SAT. JUNE 14, '86

ST. PROCOPIUS
1625 SOUTH ALLPORT
(1 BLK. WEST OF RACINE)
PROFESSIONAL SECURITY PROVIDED — DOORS OPEN 7:00
$5.00 WITH ANY FLYER DATED 6/14/86 — $6.00 WITHOUT
SUPER LIGHT & SOUND THAT WILL AMAZE YOUR EYES AND EARS
CHICAGO's MAGIC SOUNDS

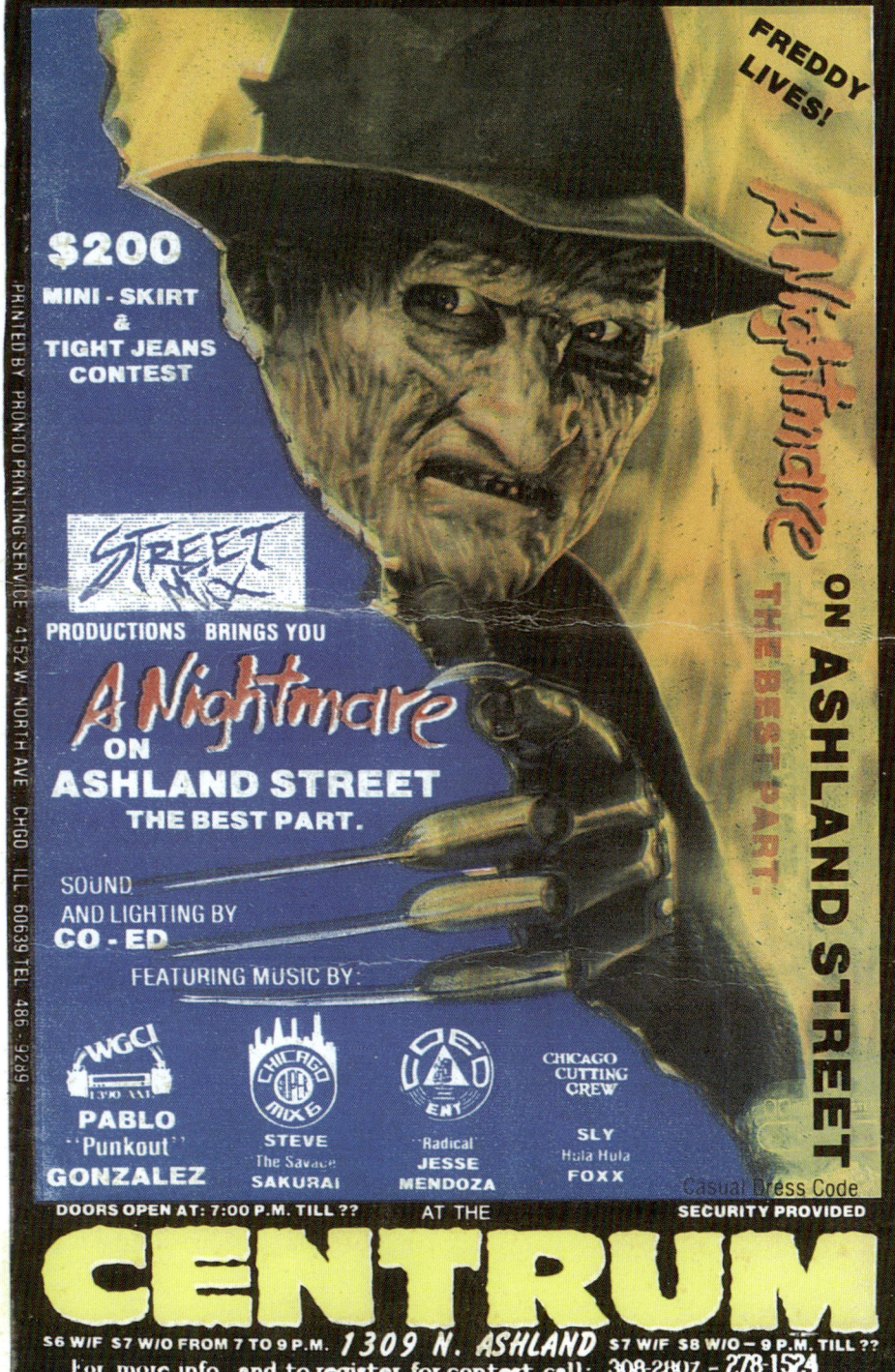

Mix Masters Present...
GET IN THE MIX IN "86"
Featuring
A HOT MIX SHOW/DANCE PARTY

JAN. 10 '86
DOORS OPEN 6 P.M. TILL 2 A.M.
PROFESSIONAL SOUNDS BY FRENCHY
PROFESSIONAL SECURITY BY APOLLO
ADMISSION: $5 W/FLYER
$7 W/OUT

WITH  **HOT MIX 5**
JULIAN "JUMPIN" PEREZ
KENNY "JAMMIN" JASON
FEATURING HIS NEW HIT SINGLE
"JAM TRACKS"
ALSO
THE MIX MASTERS
Joey "Jammin" Diaz
Martin "Boogie Man" Luna
AND GUEST APPEARANCE BY THE GROUP **QUEST**
REVIEWING THEIR NEW HIT SINGLE "MIND GAMES"
PLUS YOUR HOST BY POPULAR DEMAND —
CHICAGO'S GODFATHER OF DISCO
JESSE JONES OF **LOOP RECORDS**
GIVING AWAY **FREE RECORDS**.
FOR MORE INFO. GO TO THE DANCE

AT
THE UNION HALL
9350 South Chicago Ave.
BE THERE FOR THE BIGGEST DANCE EVER TO HIT SOUTH CHICAGO

WINDY CITY MIXERS
OUR MUSIC WILL BLOW YOU AWAY
Presents...

GET YOUR ASS ON THE FLOOR
(ASI ME GUSTA BAILA)

Featuring

HOT MIX 5, INC. **MICKEY OLIVER** *HEARD EXCLUSIVELY ON* **WBMX 102.7 FM**
"MIXIN"

CESAR ECHEVARRIA **TONY ESTRADA**
JOHN DAVIDSON   **ROBERTO CALEZ**

Plus

PERFORMING HIS YET TO BE RELEASED SINGLE
"GET YOUR ASS ON THE FLOOR"

TONY "BOOM BOOM" BADEA

WITH SPECIAL PERFORMANCE BY THE WINNER OF THE GREAT BATTLE OF THE DANCE GROUPS

A.K.A.
(ALWAYS KICKIN' ASS)

SAT. SEPT. 28, '85
CENTRUM HALL
1309 N. ASHLAND
(ASHLAND & MILWAUKEE — ACROSS FROM ZAYRES)

DOORS OPEN 8:00 TILL 2:00   CASH BAR AVAILABLE $5 W/FLYER $6 AT DOOR
SECURITY PROVIDED

PRONTO PRINTING SERVICE 4152 W. NORTH AVE. CHICAGO. ILL. 60639 TEL. 486-9289

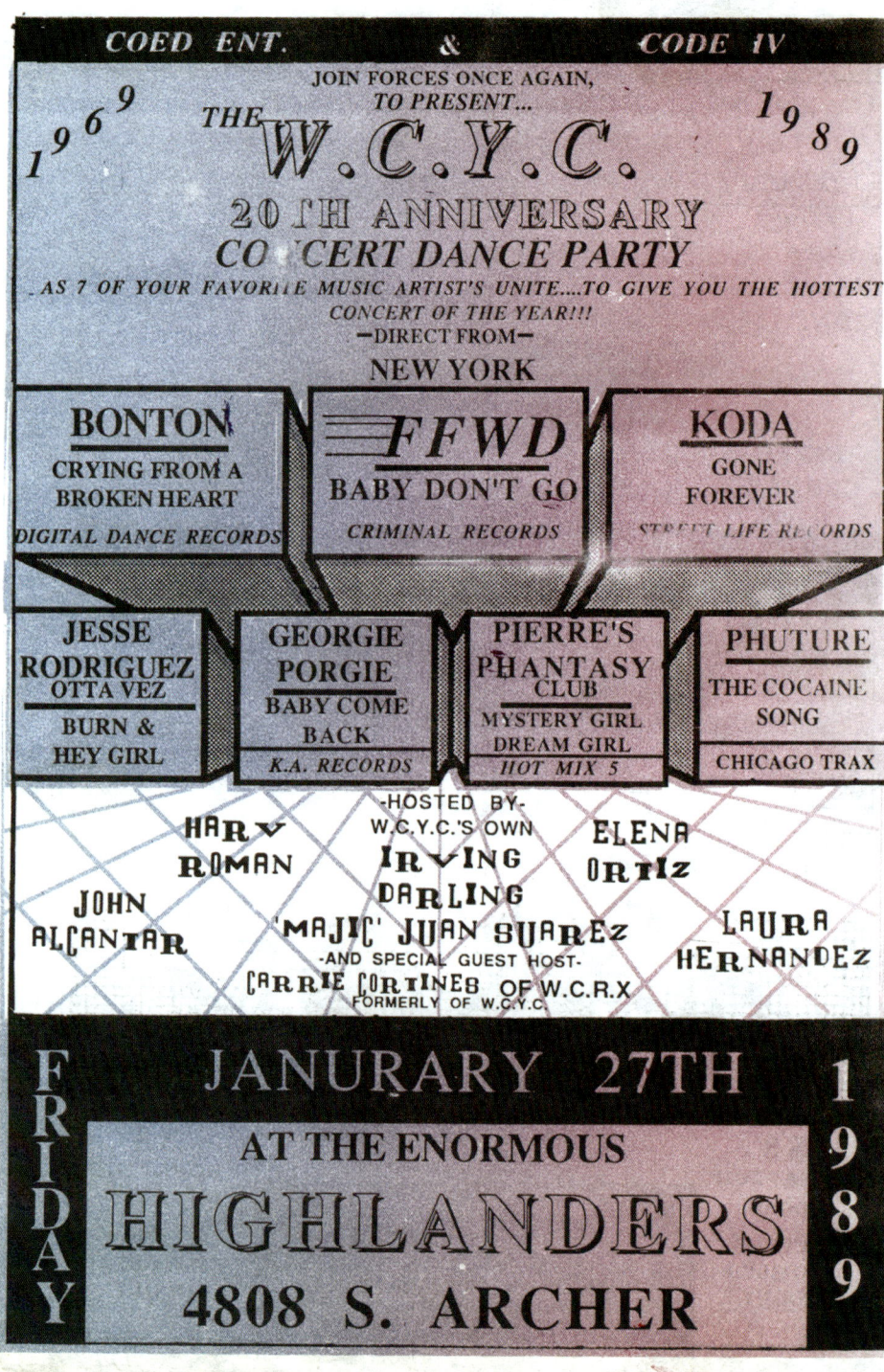

Inman and Mitchel

 monta

PRESENTS

HOUSE REVO

THE NEW BEG

SUN - APR, 22ND

Starting Spring Break

DOWNTOWN AT T
BISMARCK

171 W. Randolph

7PM - 2AM $8.0

Exclusive

...UTION
...ING

Music by:

Ron Hardy

Gene Hunt
(EXCLUSIVE MONTANA)

Boo Williams
AVILLON (EXCLUSIVE MONTANA)
& *Eric Wade*
(EXCLUSIVE MONTANA)

8:30

Dimensional *Sounds* & *High Fashion Dance*
Invite You To...

Dance, Rock, & Feel The Beat

With Native Music By
RALPHIE "THE RAZZ" ROSARIO

WBMX 102.7 FM — **HOT MIX 5, INC.**

— Also —

MIKE MARTINEZ
"NANDY"
VIRAMONTES
OZZY CHAVEZ

RICK ISAIS
CHAZ D.
RICH ROBOLINO
RUBEN FLORES

1,500 SQ. FT. OF DANCE FLOOR — SUPER SOUND & LIGHTS

COME MOVE YOUR BODY WITH THE **HOTTEST** SCHOOLS
CURIE · KELLY · RICHARDS · JUAREZ · BOGAN · MARIA
ST. JOSEPH · ST. RITA · ST. CASIMER · FARRAGUT ·
SACRED HEART

At The Perect Party

LOS GLOBOS
31ST. & CENTRAL PARK

FRI. MARCH 7, '86

COVER IS $4.00 W/H.S. — I.D. TILL 10:00 FROM 10:00 ON $5.00 W/FLYER $6.00 W/O
SECURITY BY CHGO. POLICE — DOORS OPEN AT 7:30 TILL ?? CASH BAR AVAILABLE

D.J. INTERNATIONAL RECORDING ARTIST

FILMING THEIR MUSIC VIDEO

Sat. Dec. 21

J.M. SILK

8 P.M. Til 3 A.M.

PLUS SPECIAL SURPRISE GUEST

── PLUS OPENING UP THE SHOW ──

(LIVE) **Nick H. & Co**
PREMIERING THEIR SMASH HIT "NEVER GIVE UP"

── PLUS ──

THE FABULOUS — WORLD FAMOUS

Hot Mix Five

MICKEY "MIXIN" OLIVER, FARLEY "FUNKIN" KEITH, JULIAN "JUMPIN" PEREZ, FRANKIE "HOLLYWOOD" RODRIGUEZ, RALPHI "ROCKIN" ROSARIO, AND KENNY "JAMMIN" JASON

USA RAINBO DISCO
4836 N CLARK (AT LAWRENCE)

DOORS OPEN 8 PM TIL 3 AM
WATCH FOR FURTHER DETAILS FOR INFORMATION CALL 226-9376

Tony Bitoy Productions Presents The

"FEEL SO GOOD"
CONCERT
AND
DANCE PARTY

PERFORMING 'LIVE'

Company 'B'

SINGING THEIR #1 SMASH HIT:
"FASCINATED
BY YOUR LOVE"

DANCE MUSIC BY THE ELITE MEMBER OF
Larry "Amazin" Thompson
Sly "Hula Hula" Foxx
Charlie Chaz D.
& Wen Paez

WINNERS OF THE N.Y. VS. CHICAGO
"BATTLE OF THE D-Js"

NON-STOP ENTERTAINMENT DON'T MISS IT!
For more info. phone 943-2347

SAT. MAY 2, 1987
RAINBO
4836 N. CLARK

- DOORS OPEN AT 9 P.M.
- SHOWTIME: 11 P.M.

ADMISSION
- $8 W/ ADVANCE TKTS. OR V.I.P. CARD.
- $9 WITH FLYER.
- $10 AT THE DOOR.
- ALL AGES ON THE MAIN FLOOR.
- 21 OR OLDER ON 2ND FLOOR.
- CASH BAR AVAILABLE

ADVANCE SALE TICKETS AVAILABLE AT THE FOLLOWING LOCATIONS:

ADVANCE SALE TICKETS AVAILABLE AT THE FOLLOWING LOCATIONS	
• ALL TICKETMASTER OUTLETS	• DISCO CITY No. 6 ... 2620 N. Milwaukee
• ROSE RECORDS ..... (All Locations)	• DISCO CITY No. 7 ... 3111 N. Lincoln
• CARSON PIRIE SCOTT.. (All Locations)	• DISCO CITY No. 8 ... 4042 W. North Ave.
• RAINBO BOX OFFICE ... 4836 N. Clark	• IMPORTS ETC. ... 711 S. Plymouth Court
• LOOP RECORDS ..... 320 S. State St.	• J.R's MUSIC SHOP ..... Evergreen Plaza

COMING SATURDAY, MAY 16: "THE WORLD'S BIGGEST DANCE PARTY ON NAVY PIER"

Chicago's Magic Sounds

INVITES YOU TO CELEBRATE VALENTINE'S DAY WITH

Their First Dance Concert of the Year

PERFORMING THEIR LATEST HIT..."YOU CAN DO IT" BY

MICHAELANGELO & TAMMY THOMAS

FRI. FEB. 14, 1986

GRAND MANOR

5436 W. ARCHER (CORNER OF CICERO)

FEATURING FOR THE FIRST TIME IN CHICAGO
NEW YORK'S ZULU NATION
PRESENTS

"THE VILLAGE CREW"

INCLUDING SPECIAL ATTRACTION BY

RALPHY ROSARIO & MATT WARREN

SHOW STARTS AT 11:30 SHARP
"RAZZ"
BAILA ASI ME GUSTA"
BACK BY POPULAR DEMAND
"RAZZ"
KILL YOURSELF DANCING

— PLUS —JACKING THE MOTHER F_____ HOUSE CHICAGO'S MAGIC SOUNDS OWN D.J.'S

CARLOS THE "B — BOY" BELTRAN   **RICK TORRES**
ERIK "D"   THE NEW JENALS.   **JESSE CARRILLO**
MARTINO "SPINNING" RAMOS — SLY "HULA HULA" FOXX

so come and dance the **lovers** night away as we'll BE GIVING AWAY CASSETTES RECORDED BY CHICAGO'S MAGIC SOUNDS D.J.'S

P.S. AFTER 1,000 PEOPLE DOORS WILL BE CLOSED. SO COME EARLY. AND DON'T FORGET **MARCH 1ST** AT THE **GRAND MANOR** SOMETHING **HOT..!!** THIS EVENT WILL BE VIDEO TAPED — SO PLEASE LEAVE YOUR TROUBLES AT HOME.

P.S. IF YOU MISSED RALPHIE ROSARIO'S & MATT WARREN'S LAST SHOW...DUE TO OVER CROWDNESS,
ADMISSION: $7.00 W/FLYER $8.00 W/O DOORS OPEN 7 P.M. TILL ??

INFO. CALL: **RICK TORRES** 254-4822   **CARLOS BELTRAN** 522-2103

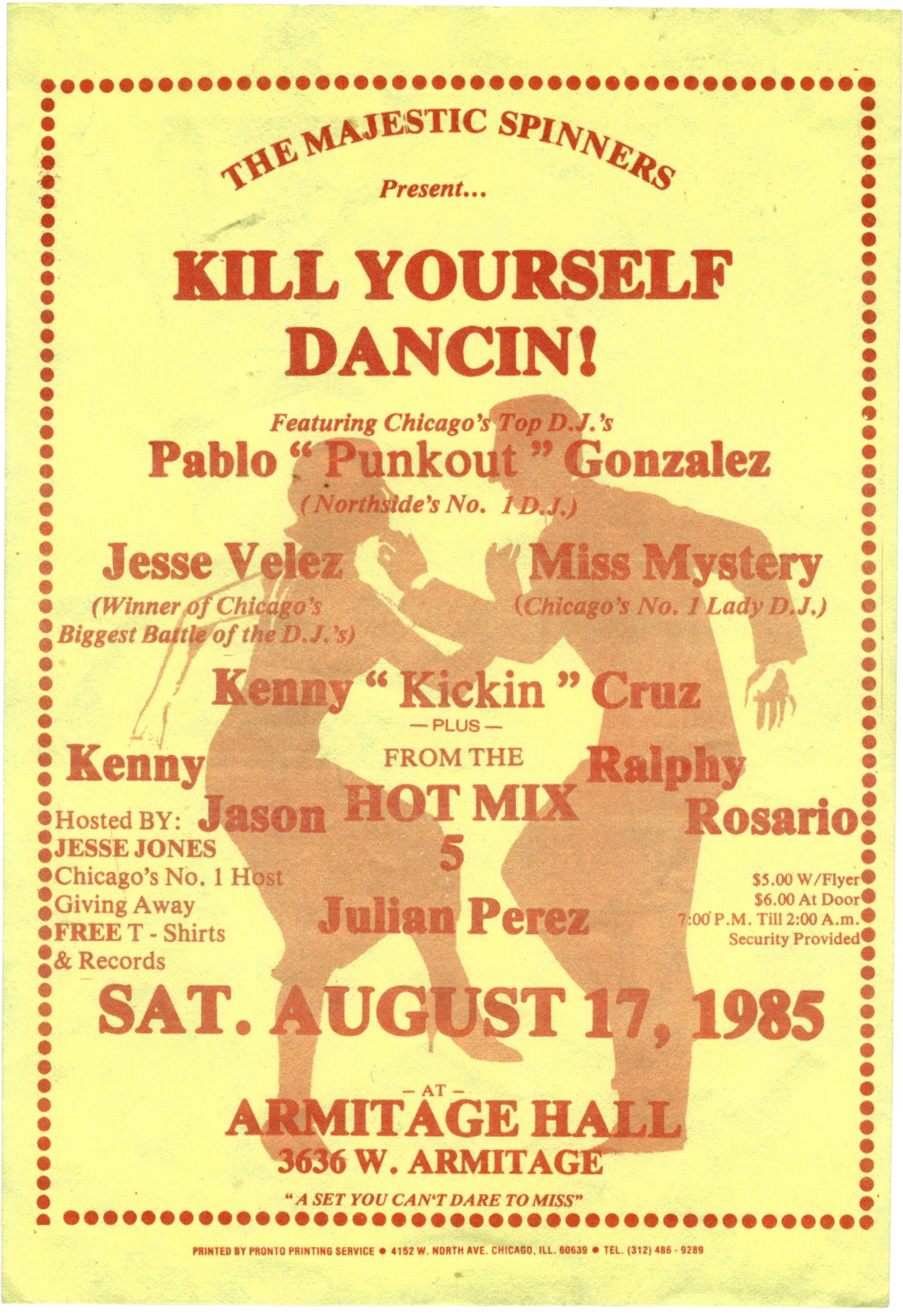

THE MAJESTIC SPINNERS
Present...
KILL YOURSELF DANCIN!
Featuring Chicago's Top D.J.'s
Pablo " Punkout " Gonzalez
(Northside's No. 1 D.J.)
Jesse Velez
(Winner of Chicago's Biggest Battle of the D.J.'s)
Miss Mystery
(Chicago's No. 1 Lady D.J.)
Kenny " Kickin " Cruz
— PLUS —
Kenny Jason
FROM THE HOT MIX 5
Ralphy Rosario
Julian Perez
Hosted BY: JESSE JONES Chicago's No. 1 Host Giving Away FREE T - Shirts & Records
$5.00 W/Flyer
$6.00 At Door
7:00 P.M. Till 2:00 A.m.
Security Provided
SAT. AUGUST 17, 1985
— AT —
ARMITAGE HALL
3636 W. ARMITAGE
"A SET YOU CAN'T DARE TO MISS"
PRINTED BY PRONTO PRINTING SERVICE • 4152 W. NORTH AVE. CHICAGO, ILL. 60639 • TEL. (312) 486 - 9289

— PLUS —

THE ULTIMATE DANCE BATTLE OF THE DECADE!!

NEW YORK VS. CHICAGO

STRAIGHT FROM MANHATTAN STRAIGHT FROM BROOKLIN   CHICAGO'S TOP DANCE GROUPS

"BODY" — N.Y NO. 1 DANCERS

"RYTHM REACTION" — "N.Y. WILDEST"

"CULITOS" — "MORE THAN JUST A DANCE GROUP"

"A.K.A." — MORE THAN YOU CAN HANDLE

BE THERE AS THE LONG AWAITED EVENT HAS ARRIVED, WILL **NEW YORK** TAKE THE WIND OUT OF THE WINDY CITY OR WILL **CHICAGO** TAKE A BITE OUT OF THE BIG APPLE? YOU HAVE TO **BE THERE** TO EXPERIENCE THIS EVENT, AS OVER 5,000 PARTY ANIMALS WILL JACK UP THE HOUSE!!

FRI. JUNE 13, '86
AT THE ARAGON
1106 W. Lawrence

"THIS IS'NT JUST A DANCE, IT'S CHICAGO'S MAIN EVENT"

$7.00 ADVANCE
$9.00 W/FLYER
10.00 AT DOOR

PROPER ATTIRE
SECURITY PROVIDED
DOORS OPEN 8 P.M. - 2 A.M.

A PABLO GONZALEZ PRODUCTION

Midnight Fantasy Dance Promotion

BRINGS TO YOU FOR THE **FIRST TIME** IN CHICAGO'S SOUTH SIDE

LIVE IN CONCERT

WHITE BOY MIKE & **BAD BOY BILL**

LIVE IN CONCERT

CONCERT BEGINS AT 10 P.M.

CONCERT BEGINS AT 10 P.M.

WBMX 102.7 FM AM 1490

HOUSE AND NEW WAVE

"THE STRENGTH"
— PERFORMING —
WATCH THE FUNKY HONEY GO!!
BUT THAT'S NOT ALL...

HECTOR & CARLOS
PERFORMING THEIR LATEST HIT
CRIMES OF LOVE

WHEN YOU THOUGHT IT WAS SAFE TO GET OFF THE DANCE FLOOR

10 OF CHICAGO'S ULTIMATE D.J.'S

RICH "Hot Mix" HUERTA	KIKE Housemaster V.	MIGUEL RODRIGUEZ	"Jack Master" JAY	MIKE "Mixin" HUERTA
GABRIEL "Rican" RODRIGUEZ	JESSE DE LA PENA	RICKY "Rockin" ALDONA	PEE WEE	NOEL "P.R." PEREZ

KICKIN THIS PARTY ON THE MIC WILL BE ELECTRIFYING SOUNDS OWN

DANCIN DION & MC 12 GAUGE

AT

BLESSED AGNES
2617 S. CENTRAL PK.
(1/2 BLOCK SOUTH OF 26TH CENTRAL PK.)

$5 W/F OR ANY H.S. I.D. UNTIL 9 P.M.
$6 AT DOOR

DOORS OPEN AT 6:30 P.M.

SAT. OCT. 22, '88

CHICAGO POLICE SECURITY   CHICAGO POLICE SECURITY

(WE RESERVE THE RIGHT TO REFUSE ANYONE)

D.C. DANCE PRODUCTIONS
Presents

LIVE IN CONCERT
M. DOC

M. DOC - PRODUCED BY STEVE "Silk" HURLEY
PERFORMING HIT SINGLES "It's Percussion", "Time To Go Go House"
AND MORE.
ALSO PERFORMING A NEW SINGLE NEVER HEARD BEFORE.
Free Records and Tapes will be given away during and after the show.
ALSO
**DANNY "Mixin" MARCIS
CHRISTY
CARLOS "Spinnin" RODRIGUEZ**
at

McGreevy's
2680 Golf Road
Glenview, Il. 60025
729-7704

FRIDAY, JUNE 23

Doors open at 7:00 • Show starts at 10:00 • $6 cover

"CHICAGO'S QUICK MIX 3" INC.

Dare You To Experience A Night Of...

JUNGLE MADNESS

As The "SAVAGE DANCERS" From The Northside Return To The Southside With Their Hottest Performance Ever!!

The CULITOS

Radar	Miritza
Tin	
Gucci	Jackie
Bobby	Evelyn
Nelson	
Alan	Joanie
Rojelio	Alma

Also

Jacking The Native Sounds For The Wild Night Will Be "The Hottest Line Up Of Chicago's D.J.'S Ever Assembled Under One Roof"!!

CHARLIE "CHAZ" D
CURIE H.S.

MARTINO "SPINNIN" RAMOS — JENALS
SLY "HULA HULA" FOX — JENALS

FERNANDO "NANDY" VIRAMONTES
KELLY H.S.

VAL RODRIGUEZ — J.V.M.
JOSE ROMERO — W.C.Y.C.

RICHIE "BE BAD" ROBOLINO
CURIE H.S.

JAVIER LEBRON — ST. RITA H.S.
PEPE QUINTANA — HUBBAD H.S.

WILSON "VICIOUS" VEGA
DANCING WHEELS

MICKEY "D" — DANCING WHEELS
TOM PEREZ — JUAREZ H.S.

FRI. FEB. 21, '86
SACRED HEART HALL
4619 S. WOLCOTT

$5.00 W/FLYER $6.00 W/O

Hosted By: **PAUL "PUMPIN" BARREDA** — MIX PRODUCTION

ATTENTION!! **ATTENTIION!!** **ATTENTION!!**

WE WILL BE GIVING AWAY FREE TICKETS TO THE "WORLD'S SUPER DANCE" FEB. 22 AT THE ARAGON. WE WILL ALSO BE GIVING AWAY FREE T-SHIRTS. FREE RECORDS. FREE CASSETTES.

FOR MORE INFO. CALL: RICH R. 776-1093 OR BETO G. AT 376-4029

P.S. THIS PARTY IS GUARANTEED TO BRING OUT THE ANIMAL INSIDE YOU FOR A NIGHT OF UNFORGETABLE ENTERTAINMENT!!!

6:00 P.M. TILL ???

PROFESSIONAL SECURITY PROVIDED ALL NIGHT INSIDE AND OUT

Chicago's Dance Promotions AND **CHICAGO'S ENTERTAINMENT** PRESENTS...

TEAMS UP TO BRING YOU CHICAGO'S NO. 1'S MAIN EVENT!!

THE MOBILE DISCO MATCH UP.

D.J.'S COMPETING FOR A GIGANTIC 7 FOOT TROPHY

BATTLE BEGINS AT 10:00 P.M. SHARP

ALL BREAKERS WELCOME!!

SOUTH, NORTH, EAST & WEST

WITH A SPECIAL APPEARANCE BY: **"LOURDES"** WINNER OF THE BATTLE OF THE LADY D.J.'S

PLUS! A SUPER LIGHT SHOW!

FEATURING: CHICAGO'S CITY WIDE HOTTES MUSIC MASTERS

FELIX CARRANZA OF CHICAGO'S DANCE PROMOTIONS	DAVE CHACON OF MAGIC SOUNDS	MATT WARREN OF SUNSET MOBILE DISCO	TONY BADEA OF MAGIC MIXERS	LEE CASTLE OF MIDNIGHT EXPRESS	PEDRO PEREZ OF MADE 'N HEAVEN DISCO	LOUIE ORPEZA OF FANTASY	CARLOS BELTRAN OF MAGIC SOUNDS

P.S. COMING SOON...CHICAGO'S ENTERTAINMENT TEAMS UP ONCE AGAIN TO BRING YOU A SPECTACULAR SHOW! NOW GET READY FOR BOY GEORGE LIVE ON STAGE COMING SOON...

SECURITY PROVIDED
DOORS OPEN 8 P.M. TILL ?
$5.00 W/FLYER $7.00 AT DOOR

SAT. JUNE 9, '84 AT THE WESTERN AVENUE BALLROOM 3504 S. WESTERN

YOUR HOST JESSE & TONY

LAST CHANCE TO PARTY BEFORE SUMMER VACATION...ALSO SEE REVERSE SIDE TO MAIN EVENT!!

CHICAGO PART
MORE THAN JU
FRIDAY, FEB
A.C. CLUB
LIVE IN CONCERT: A LINEUP OF

FOR MORE INFO CALL 942-1431

RANDOM DRAWING FOR FREE LIMO RIDE!

RALPHIE ROSARIO

BAILIE
AMOR PUERTORIQUENO
I WANT YOUR LOVE IN THE NIGHT

SPANKY

CAN U FEEL THE BASS
WE ARE THE PHUTURE

PLUS $500 M.C.

D.J. PIERRE & PFANTASY CLUB

ALSO FEATURING C
BAD BOY BILL • JULIAN "JUMPIN
MIKE "HITMAN" WILSON • STEVE
JACK MASTER JAY • TONY

GUEST
D. J. SMURF • ORLANDO "COOL OUT"
ALEX "NONSTOP" GA

HOSTED BY HARV ROMAN & CARY CORTINEZ

COME AND BE PART OF TH

...TERS PRESENT
... DANCE PART 2
...Y 24, AT THE
...AUKEE & PULASKI
...O'S BEST HOUSE PERFORMERS.

6:30 TO ??
$9.00 With Flyer
$10.00 Without Flyer

...KATHERINE
TAKE MY LOVE

MICKEY OLIVER & PATRIS
NEVER LET GO
IN-TEN-SI-T
JACKIN' NATIONAL ANTHEM
I NEED A BEAT

...VS. FATMAN $500

VIS 'a VIS
(LIVE FROM NY)

LISTEN TO: WCRX-FM • WGCI-AM • WCYC-FM

...'S "HOTTEST" D.J.'S
... • GABRIEL "RICAN" RODRIGUEZ
...E" SAKURAI • RICK "THE RIPPER"
...BOOM" BADEA • FATMAN "T"

...CLUDE:
... • WONDERBOY WUL • TITO "2 HOT" H
...UTRAGEOUS OLLIE V

...CURITY PROVIDED BY F.I.S.T. & CHICAGO POLICE

...T PARTY AT THE A.C. CLUB!

Lady Luck Production
Invites You To
THE

HOTTEST SET IN CHICAGO 1986

Featuring
Chicago's Best Hot Mix 5 Own
KENNY "JAMMIN" JASON

SUPER LIGHT & SOUND   **SUPER LIGHT & SOUND**

WBMX 102.7 FM

CHARLIE CHAZ D. **HECTOR FRIAS** **NANDY VIRAMONTES**
OF   OF   OF
QUICK 3 MIX   NIGHT SOUND   NIGHT SOUND

SPECIAL GUEST
FUNK BOYS & GIRLS

FELIX CARRANZA
OF
CHICAGO ENTERTAINMENT

A LIVE PERFORMANCE BY
IMPORTED TASTE
(DANCER)

FRI. MARCH 7, '86
SACRED HEART HALL
4619 S. WOLCOTT ST.

$6.00 AT DOOR — $5.00 W/THIS FLYER OR ANY OTHER DANCE FLYER THAT IS ON THIS DAY.
DOORS OPEN 7:30 P.M. TILL ?? — SECURITY PROVIDED — ALL DANCE GROUPS AND PARTY ANIMALS ARE WELCOMED.
THIS IS GOING TO BE THE HOTTEST DANCE OF THE YEAR. SO BE READY TO JACK THAT BODY WITH CHICAGO BEST, BECAUSE WE CAN'T STOP THE BEAT!!

Technics
AMERICAN D.J. MIXING CHAMPIONSHIPS
NORTHSIDE AND SOUTHSIDE REGIONALS

DMC 1989 DJ INTERNATIONAL

LISTEN TO W.C.Y.C. (90.5 FM), AM 1390 W.G.C.I. AND W.C.R.X.
FOR MORE INFO. AND YOUR CHANCE TO WIN FREE TICKET GIVEAWAYS...

SAT. FEB. 11
AT THE LUXURIOUS
CEZAR'S INN
5001 W. 79th St.
(2 Blocks West of Cicero)

- DOORS OPEN AT 7:00 P.M. • BATTLE STARTS AT 9:00 P.M. SHARP
- WE PARTY TILL 1:00 IN THE MORNING
- ADMISSION $8.00 WITH THIS FLYER

SR. **ORANGE CRUSH** PROD.
PRESENTS...

A PARTY CREW GET-TO-GETHER

FEATURING THE SOUNDS OF:

TELLY "THE KID" CARABALLO

CHARLIE CHAZ "D"
D.J. TEAM

MARTINO "SPINNIN'" RAMOS

FERNANDO NANDY VIRAMONTES (CBB)

RADICAL JES (COED)

FURIOUS FREDDY (TUF)

"SMOKIN'" JAV (ORANGE CRUSH)

EDGAR DYNAMITE Del Valle (TUF)

LOUIE R. (ORANGE CRUSH)

MARTIN GARCIA (NITE LIFE)

AIR CONDITIONED

REFRESHMENTS WILL BE SERVED

JULY 10, 1987
GOLD COAST INN
(71st MAPLEWOOD)

8:00 P.M. TIL ???   8:00 P.M. TIL ???

HOSTED BY: *Rick Torres* MIKE, B B, & JAV

$5.00 W/FLYER $6.00 W/OUT $4.00 W/TICKETS

SPECIAL INVITATIONS TO: ALL STARS, UPP, FBZ, FGZ, SPP, LT'S, PKC, WANDERERS, KAAOS, KPP, GQ, TBZ, COED, DESTINEE, PCB

ALL PARTY CREWS MUST CONTACT MIKE AT: 247-0448, JAV 436-2738 FOR ADVANCE TICKETS AND INFO.

GUEST D.J'S OF THAT HOT NIGHT

PEP "PRINCE OF HOUSE) (VOL. 1)
"SWEET BOY" DAVID (VOL. 1)
ZIGSTER (VOL. 1)
ANDRES LOPEZ (C.H.S.)

ALEX PEREZ (L.T.C.)
MARIO LUNA (L.T.C.)
ADAM "ROCK" (C.P.S.)
JUNIOR (KAAOS)

WE BRING TO YOU CHICAGO'S CRAZIEST PARTY CREW

LATIN TASTE
Hosted By: POKEY & QUEMADO

IN THE HOTTEST SPOT IN WAUKEGAN

ST. JOSEPH HALL
405 W. BELVIDERE
SAT. MARCH 21, '87

SECURITY PROVIDED
$7 W/FLYER AND $8.00 W/O
DOORS OPEN AT 7:00 P.M

SOUND & LIGHTING BY:
MIDNIGHT JAMMERS

INMAN AND MITCHELLO'S EXCLUSIVE

MONTANA

EASTER EVE
SAT APRIL 1

CLASSIC - HOUSE - CO

(PROMOTORS AW

DOWNTOWN

AT THE

PALMER HOUSE

STATE STREET AT MONROE
(CTA TRANS.) DAN RYAN A OR B - GET OFF
AT ADAMS AND WABASH WALK 1 BLOCK
NORTH OF WABASH....................

Come early when the party get's packed no more will be let
Who's the best — Who's most popular — You choose

D.J.--

Promoter..

Montana - 1989 McCormick & Photon popular place Award
Lil Louis — 1989 Bismarck most popular place - Award
Ron Hardy - Godfather of true House - Award
Lil Louis - 1989 Medusa's 2ND most popular place - Award
Gucci - 1989 Hyde PK. Racquet Ball club popular place - Award
Chicago Bad Boys - most Valuable promoter - Award
WKKC - Only Deep House Station - Award

IN ASSOCIATION WITH I.P.E.

7PM til 2AM
$6.00 til 8PM

CALL
488 - 0526

TH
VENTION
(REMONY)

MUSIC BY:
ERIC WADE
Terry Hunter
Boo Williams
Armando
Pharris
Chris Underwood
Gene Hunt
NEW COMER **Ace**
Jamile Patton
(Mr. Malcom X -Himself)

JUST US GIRLZ
INVITES YOU TO
PARADISE HALL
1748 W. 48th & WOOD
SAT. DEC. 10, 1988

BRINGING YOU SOME OF CHICAGO'S TOP D.J.'S

SPINNING THEIR BEST IN

FEATURING

POWER MAXIMUM

TELLY "SUPERMIX KIDD"
RICK TORRES
RAPHAEL "ITO" GARCIA

CESAR HERNANDEZ
CARLOS HEREIDA
BADD EXAMPLES

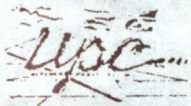

TONY GARCIA
CARLOS CASTILLO
LATIN SOCIETY

MARIO "LIVE IT UP" LUNA
JOSE GUESS MAN FLORES
"MANIAC" MAURICIO

MAD - HOUSE
MIGUEL

ROY "BAD BOY"
ABEL G.

JESSE DE LA PENA

GUEST D.J.'S
CHICO, NINO & ALFONSO

PLUS A SPECIAL PERFORMANCE BY CHICAGO'S VERY OWN

EURO DANCERS

P.S. HAPPY BIRTHDAY TO MABEL, JENNY, & PATTY (CONGRATULATIONS)

SPECIAL INVITATION TO: O.T.B., BADD EXAMPLES, UPPZ, FB'Z AND GIRLZ, UPC, OK, OUTCAST, STYLISTICS, COED, OC'S, NBZ AND GIRLS, UNTOUCHABLES, LTC, LIC, MPC, X - TACY, LSC, HOUSE DOGS, WHITE KNIGHTS, SOPHISTICATED LADIES.

$5.00 WITH ANY FLYER ON THIS DATE
$6.00 W/F
$7.00 W/O

DOORS OPEN AT 7 P.M.
REFRESHMENTS AVAILABLE

SOUND & LIGHTING BY:

WE RESERVE THE RIGHT TO REFUSE ANYONE.   SECURITY PROVIDED

Night Sounds Prom. presents...

LET'S ALL CHANT

N.S.P.

DANCE TO THE SULTRY SOUNDS OF...
CHICAGO'S "HOTTEST" MUSIC MIXERS

HECTOR "FREAKIN" FRIAS   FERNANDO "NANDY" VIRAMONTES
FELIX CARRANZA   LOUIE OROPEZA
LUIS VALENCIA   MARK SANTANA

SAT. MAY 18, '85

AT THE

GRAND MANOR
5436 W. ARCHER AVE.

$6.00 W/F
$7.00 W/OUT

— ALSO —
INTRODUCING
THE MAGNETIC SENSUAL MOVES OF THE UNIQUE
KRAZY KREW ROCKERS & WINDY CITY KREW

DOORS OPEN AT 8:00 P.M.

200 SUMMER SHIRTS "FREE" FOR THE FIRST 200 PEOPLE TO ARRIVE AT THE DOOR

SOUND SYSTEM BY: N.S.P.'S HIGH TECH MUSIC INC.
THE POWER OF MUSIC YOU'LL EVER EXPERIENCE

PRINTED BY PRONTO PRINTING SERVICE ● 4152 W. NORTH AVE. CHICAGO, ILL. 60639 ● TEL. (312) 486-9289

— FEATURING —
14 OF THE BEST
PARTY CREWS D.J.'S
SPINNING OFF

"Get Down" **Gilbert Avilez** **SPP**	"Pee Wee" of **LATIN TASTE**
"Smokin Jav" of **ORANGE CRUSH**	**Mike "Mixin"** **Huerta** **K - TOWN** **PARTY PEOPLE**
"Rudy Romero" of **THEE BOYZ OF 45th**	Mix - Master Micco of **PARTY CREW BOYZ**
? of **ONE THE BOYZ**	Javier Lebron of **FUNK - BOYZ**
"Guilty" **Gil** of **UNDERCOVER PARTY - PEOPLE**	David Shen of **PARTY PLAYERS OF 36**
Carlos Santillan of **KAAOS**	? of **LATIN IMAGE**
Joe of **G.Q.**	Radical Jes of **C.O.E.D.**

AND ALSO TROWING DOWN IN THE G .... CONTEST

FEATURING

ORANGE CRUSH	LATIN IMAGE	STYLISTICS	KAOS
G.Q. CREW	UNDERCOVER PARTY PEOPLE	FUNK BOYZZ	PARTY CREW BOYZZ
PARTY PLAYERS OF 36th	LATIN TASTE	OTB	THE BOYZ 45th

AND TO KEEP YOUR NALGAS MOVING WITH THE SOUNDS OF

MIGUEL RODRIGUEZ
TONY G.
JAN OLMEDO
JAZZIN JOE

RICH MARTINEZ
CHAZ D.
FAST MOVIN
FRAUSTO
DANCIN DION

Chicago Sound Promoters
BRINGS YOU ANOTHER DISCO EXTRAVAGANZA!!!

HOUSE REUNION 1990
SAT. MAR. 31st at
The RIVIERA
4647 N. Broadway
(AT LAWRENCE)

HOSTED BY:
WGCI 107.5FM AM1390
89.3 WKKC PINK HOUSE &
107.5 WGCI RAMONSKI LUV

BRINGING YOU THE SOUNDS OF PLEASURE WILL BE:

RON HARDY   **PHARRIS THOMAS**

CHRIS UNDERWOOD   **GENE HUNT**

TERRY HUNTER   **ARMANDO**

SATURDAY, MARCH 31st

THIS WILL BE THE LARGEST HOUSE PARTY IN CHICAGO HISTORY, SO MARK YOUR CALENDER....

17 & OLDER TO PARTY,................GEN. ADM.. $8.00

21 & OLDER TO DRINK ....8:00–p.m. till 4:00–a.m.

P.S. WE'VE SEARCHED FOR THE RIGHT CLUB(NOT HOTEL) TO HAVE THIS EVENT, THE SEARCH IS OVER, and YOU'LL LOVE IT!

TONY BITOY PRODUCTIONS PRESENTS
RAINBO's 3RD ANNIVERSARY PARTY

THANK YOU CHICAGO. FOR 3 YEARS WE'VE JACKED-THE BOX AT RAINBO ON SAT. NITE. AND WE'RE STILL No. 1 COME & CELEBRATE WITH US.

DANCE MUSIC BY

CHICAGO'S OPREM D.J. TEAM

- Larry "AMAZIN" Thompson
- SLY "Hula Hula" FOXX
- CHARLIE CHAZ D.

LISTEN TO **WBMX 102.7 FM** FOR MORE INFO.

PLUS A SEXY DANCE PERFORMANCE BY THE FAMOUS

CULITO DANCERS

SAT. JAN. 10, 1987
AT THE RAINBO
4836 N. CLARK

ADMISSION $4 W/TONY BITOY VIP CARD $5 W/FLYER $6 W/O
DOOR OPEN AT 9 P.M. TILL ??? FOR MORE INFO. Call 943-2347
COMING FEB. 7 THE N.Y. vs. CHI. BATTLE OF THE D.J's.

BENEFIT DANCE

THURSDAY
OCT. 26, 1989

Dance Party Featu[ring]

KOOL R[OCK]
ADAM

Music Provided By:

Cesar H.
Carlos H.

Hosted By: TROY

U P C

Raphael G.
Mario Luna

...ecial Appearance By:

THURSDAY
OCT. 26, 1989

BENEFIT DANCE

STEADY

Ricky G.
Danny "The Wild One"

Party Society

Hosted By: CHICO (The Snake)

...K

Clarence "Pumps" Perez
Arthur "Apple Jack" Monreal

POWER PRODUCTION PRESENTS

STEVE "Silk" HURLEY
IN CONCERT
WORK IT OUT

D.J. MIKE "HITMAN" WILSON

D.J. JUNGLE JORGE SUAREZ

17 & UP TO PARTY!   21 & UP TO DRINK!

SUNDAY, OCT, 1st 89
RIVIERA
DANCE CLUB Broadway & Lawrence

DOORS OPEN AT 8:00 – WE PARTY TILL 3:00 A.M.
ADMISSION $10.00 AT THE DOOR.
FOR PARTY INFO PHONE 856-0333
HOSTED BY TONY BITOY & XAVIER

YAKS IS BACK!

112th. and Michigan Ave.
½ Blk. east

Chicagos First Exclusive Young Adult Center

BEGINING
FRIDAY NOV. 8th & SATURDAY NOV. 9th
7pm til 12am

JULIAN
CORLISS
FENGER
MORGAN PARK
HARLAN
HIRSCH
C.V.S.
ROBESON
BOWEN
SIMEON
ENGLEWOOD
SOUTH SHORE
KENWOOD ACD.
HYDE PARK
CALUMET
LINDBLOOM
CARVER
GAGE PARK
TILDEN
JONES COMM.
HARPER
DUSABLE
PHILLIPS
DUNBAR
KING
HILLCREST
METRO
WHITNEY YOUNG
FLOWERS
CRETE MONETE
ACD. OF OUR LADY
ELIZABETH SETON
MENDEL
LEO
MT. CARMEL
HALES
UNITY
MOTHER MCCAULEY
QUIGLEY SOUTH
ST. LAWRENCE
CATHEDRAL
ST. ANNE'S H.S.
JOSEPHINUM
ST. MELS
ST. IGNATIUS
HOLY FAMILY
De La Salle
ST. RITA

For Mature Young Adults

Music by: **W.B.M.X. HOT MIX 5's**
Farley "Jack Master" Funk
and
Steve "J.M. Silk" Hurley

ALSO... **W.G.C.I. MASTERMIXER**
Hudson "Hot Mix" Beauduy

* ALSO SPECIAL ATTRACTION *
Chip Eberhart
The maker of
'Time To Jack'

CHICAGO's LARGEST DANCE FLOOR
Super Blasting Sounds
PROF. SECURITY (Inside & Out)

Fantastic Laser Lites
LRG. SNACK BAR
Live Concerts   Celebrity Guest
Plus A Whole Lot More

$3.00 till 10 w/Plugger

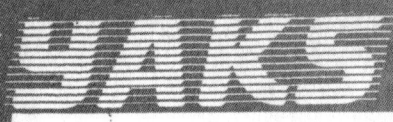

FREE ADMISSION W/ MEMBERSHIP CARDS

PePe's	Mc Donald's	112 ST.	Wendy's
	YAKS Free Parking		Michigan Ave.

NAME_____ SCHOOL_____

JR'S MUSIC SHOP · TRAX RECORDS · The Source! WCRX 88.1 FM

**SINGING THEIR SMASH HITS!!
NEVER HAS ALL OF CHICAGO BECOME UNIFIED UNDER ONE ROOF!!**

CONCERTS · CONCERTS

FINGERS INC.
"BRINGING DOWN THE WALLS"
"WASHING MACHINE"

HOUSE BEAT BOYZ

XAVIER GOLD
"YOU USED TO HOLD ME"
PRODUCED BY RALPHIE ROSARIO

FARLEY "JACKMASTER" FUNK
"THE GODFATHER OF HOUSE NATION"
SPECIAL GUEST STAR

DANNY SWEET D. WILSON
"COMMUNICATE"

JUNGLE WONZ
"TIME MARCHES ON"

HOUSE NATION · HIGH ENERGY

**JOINING FORCES FOR THE FIRST TIME:
REPRESENTATING THE HOUSE NATION:
AND REPRESENTING HIGH ENERGY DANCE MUSIC:**

HUDSON "HOT MIX" BEAUDUY · ROBERT OWENS · TYREE · MARTINO "SPINNIN" RAMOS · CHARLIE CHAZ "D" · MARTIN "BOOGIEMAN" LUNA

THIS EVENT WILL BE HOSTED BY NONE OTHER THAN - JUAN TOVAR

Free Records and T—Shirts Given Away From J.R.'s
Security Provided By **APPOLLO** And Chicago's Finest
P.S. IT'S AIR CONDITIONED!
FOR INFO. CALL: 247-0445 (LE CHIC FASHIONS).

FRI. JUNE 19, '87

TONY BITOY PRODUCTIONS PRESENTS

Chicago -vs- L.A.
BATTLE OF THE D.J.'S

FOR THE FIRST TIME IN HISTORY! THE WEST COAST BEST D.J.'S BATTLE AGAINST CHICAGO'S HOTTEST D.J.'S

HOSTED BY:

FARLEY "JACK MASTER" FUNK (WBMX 102.7 FM)

AFRIKA ISLAM (ZULU NATION'S SON OF BAM BATA)

"BAD BOY" BILL (W.B.M.X. SUPER MIX 61)

EVIL E. ("THE RHYME SYNDICATE D.J.'S") (102.7 FOR ICE T)

JULIAN "JUMPIN" PEPEZ (W.B.M.X. SUPER MIX)

D.J. ALADIN (K. DAY SPIN MASTERS)

WEN PAEZ (CHICAGO SUPREME DJ TEAM)

HENRY G. (K. DAY SPIN MASTERS)

RAINBO
4836 N. CLARK

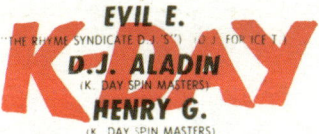

YOU HAVE TO SEE IT TO BELIVE IT!
SAT MAY 28

- FOR MORE INFO PH 856-0333
- DOORS OPEN AT 9:00 PM
- ADVANCE TICKETS $8.00
- $10.00 AT DOOR
- ALL AGES WELCOMED

$8.00 ADVANCE SELL TICKETS AVAILABLE AT THE FOLLOWING LOCATIONS
- RAINBO BOX OFFICE......4836 N. CLARK
- DISCO CITY NO. 6...2620 N. MILWAUKEE
- IMPORTS ETC..711 S. PLYMOUTH COURT
- MAC'S RECORD......5425 W. MADISON
- JR'S MUSIC SHOP....EVERGREEN PLAZA

TICKETMASTER
CARSON PIRIE SCOTT, SPORTMART, ROSE RECORDS, & SELECTED BERGNER'S
(312) 559-1212

FOR MORE **BATTLE** INFO PHONE
856-0333

PRINTED BY THE ALL NEW **SUPERULTA PRINTERS** MARTINO RAMOS & RICK TORRES (312) 927-3310

An IZZY M. and DAVID T. Production

Come One Come All and Party with the All New Ultimate Party Crew

All the Hottest and Freshest House &

Latin Breeze D.J. Carlos Herrera

New Wave Dance Music and U.P.C.'s Very Own D.J.'s MARIO LUNA RAPHAEL GARCIA

Stylistic Sounds D.J. José Muñiz

SAT. JAN. 16, 1988

$4.00 with flyer - $5.00 w/o - From 7:00 p.m. till ?

ST. PETER and PAUL Church Hall

3745 S. PAULINA

Special Invitation to all Party Crews and Especially to all you Candy Girls out there
--- SECURITY PROVIDED ---
Food and Refreshments Available ● Parking in Rear

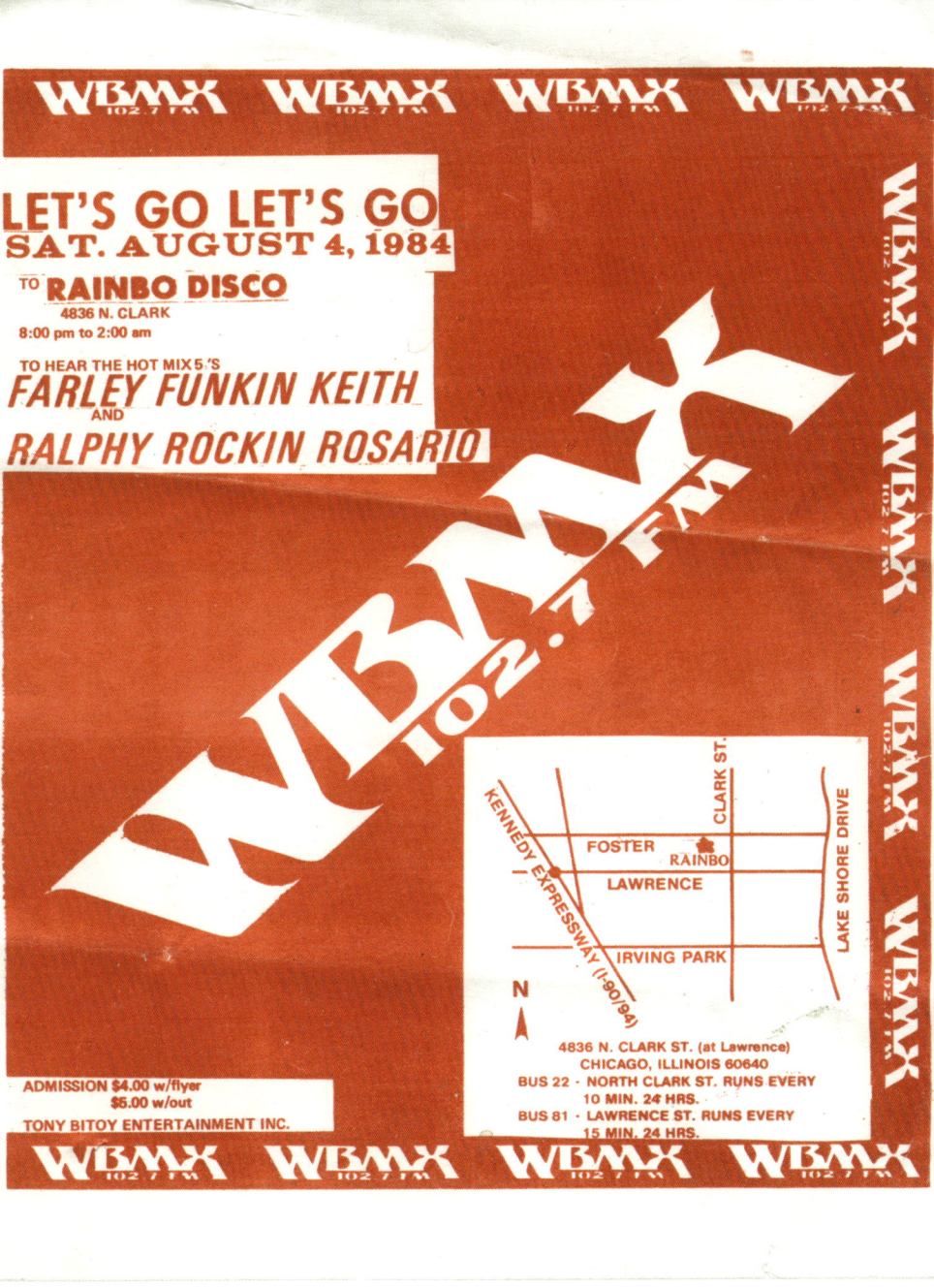

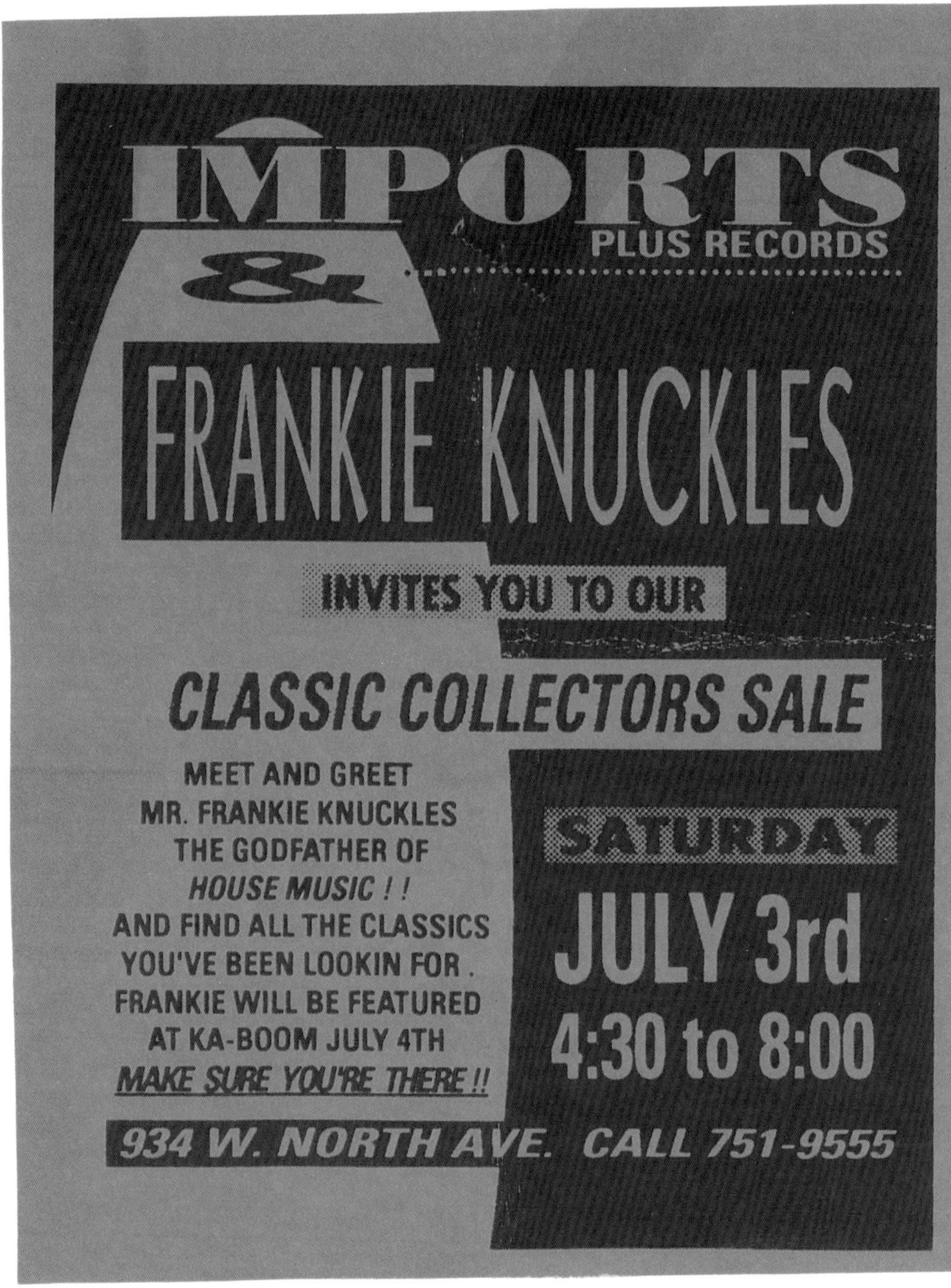

IMPORTS PLUS RECORDS &

FRANKIE KNUCKLES

INVITES YOU TO OUR

CLASSIC COLLECTORS SALE

MEET AND GREET
MR. FRANKIE KNUCKLES
THE GODFATHER OF
HOUSE MUSIC !!
AND FIND ALL THE CLASSICS
YOU'VE BEEN LOOKIN FOR.
FRANKIE WILL BE FEATURED
AT KA-BOOM JULY 4TH
<u>MAKE SURE YOU'RE THERE !!</u>

SATURDAY
JULY 3rd
4:30 to 8:00

934 W. NORTH AVE. CALL 751-9555